#4

THE DARIO QUINCY
ACADEMY OF DANCE

Twin
DANGERS

THE DARIO QUINCY
ACADEMY OF DANCE

#4

Twin
DANGERS

BY MEGAN ATWOOD

darbycreek

MINNEAPOLIS

Darby Creek
A division of Lerner Publishing Group, Inc.
241 First Avenue North
Minneapolis, MN 55401 U.S.A.

Website address: www.lernerbooks.com

Cover and interior photographs © Val Thoermer/Getty Images (main);
© iStockphoto.com/Selahattin BAYRAM (paper background).

Main body text set in Janson Text LT Std 12/17.5.
Typeface provided by Linotype AG.

Library of Congress Cataloging-in-Publication Data

Atwood, Megan.
   Twin dangers / by Megan Atwood.
      pages   cm. — (The Dario Quincy Academy of Dance ; #4)
   ISBN 978–1–4677–0933–0 (lib. bdg. : alk. paper)
   ISBN 978–1–4677–1630–7 (eBook)
   [1. Dance—Fiction. 2. Haunted places—Fiction. 3. Supernatural—Fiction.
4. Twins—Fiction. 5. Sisters—Fiction.] I. Title.
PZ7.A8952Tw 2013
[Fic]—dc23   2013000650

Manufactured in the United States of America
1– BP— 7/15/13

T⋯⋯, for their constant support.
An⋯ ⋯atrick, who literally held me up when I
⋯⋯l down. My love and gratitude to you.

Chapter 1

Sophie sighed and whispered to Emma: "I wish Trey would do a pas de deux with me *outside* of class, if you know what I mean."

She smiled at her sister, expecting a big laugh. As Sophie's twin, Emma was obligated to laugh, even if the line wasn't funny. It was the code. Twins stuck by each other no matter what. Even if that meant laughing at lame jokes.

And anyway, Sophie had been remarkably restrained on the Trey front lately. Whenever she spoke with Emma, she tried hard to not only talk about him—and that meant something, because Sophie was the talkative twin. Come to think of it, over the last week, Emma had gotten even quieter anytime Sophie talked about Trey. Maybe Sophie *had* laid it on too thick.

Still, Emma had to follow the code. She was supposed to put up with her sister, no matter how annoying Sophie got.

No laugh came from Emma, so Sophie elbowed her.

"Wha—?" Emma said. "Oh, yeah. Pas de deux."

She continued to take off her pointe shoes, then put on her blue Uggs—Sophie had the pink pair—pulling them up and positioning them perfectly on her legs.

Sophie slipped off her own pointe shoes and saw Emma sneak a peek at Trey.

Then she saw Trey sneak a peek at Emma.

Sophie shook it off.

The academy was on a break from performing any ballets. They'd just finished *Giselle*, and things had gone a little wonky—one of Sophie's best friends had almost died during the performance—so Madame Puant had decided to ease off on performances for a while. Which, in Sophie's opinion, was a good idea. She had seen her share of weird things happen at the academy, and she needed a break from any sort of intrigue. So she was happy that ballet class consisted of practicing parts from different ballets instead of working so hard toward one performance. The last two weeks, the dancers had been practicing parts from *Swan Lake*, and every girl in the company got her chance to play the lead, Odette and Odile. Every boy got to play the prince.

Which meant a lot of pas de deuxes. And Sophie could not *wait* for her pas de deux with Trey. If the academy were putting on an actual performance, she would have never gotten the chance. The student body was 4–1 girls to guys, so the same guys tended to get the lead roles. And competition among the girls was so intense that Sophie never got the lead. This was the one way she could finally dance with Trey without all the anxiety of an upcoming performance or competition from the other dancers.

Emma already had danced the pas de deux with him, and Sophie had to admit it had been beautiful. She'd tried hard not to be jealous as they acted out the love between Odette and the prince. And she kept reminding herself that it was fake.

It was just a dance.

Sophie reminded herself again that Emma knew how much she liked Trey. And they were twins—there was a code about boys too. Still, she couldn't help but feel a little uneasy about the looks Trey and Emma were giving each other.

Emma stood up and shook her legs out. Of the two of them, Emma was the more careful one, the one who always looked before she leapt. She even moved slower—each movement was deliberate and precise, in dancing and in real life. Emma was a good dancer because of this precision, but her lack of spontaneity kept her in the "good" category rather than the "great" category. For Sophie, it was the opposite. She was spontaneous and free with her emotions, but not as good at the technical stuff.

Sophie tried hard not to roll her eyes at the slowness of Emma's after-practice routine. But she couldn't help herself from saying, "We need to hurry up and get breakfast."

She looked over at Ophelia, Kayley, and Madeleine, who were looking back at the twins, clearly waiting for the two of them to join the group and head down to the dining hall.

Without looking at her, Emma said, "You go ahead. I'll be down in a minute. I need to talk to Madame."

"About what?"

"About *something*," Emma said, frustration written over her face.

"Yeah, I gathered that much. But what are you going to talk about?"

"I don't have to tell you everything, you know!" Emma yanked her bag up from the floor and stormed out, passing Madame Puant as she went.

Sophie was flabbergasted. What had just happened? She noticed that Trey was leaving in a hurry too.

Before she could think about it, though, Madeleine, Kayley, and Ophelia came over.

"So . . . that was weird," Ophelia said.

Kayley, chomping on some gum, added, "Yeah, what was that all about? Usually you guys can't even breathe without each other."

Sophie sighed. Kayley always made cracks like that. Sophie suspected she was jealous that the twins had each other—Kayley only had four brothers.

Sophie shrugged and tried to look nonchalant. "I have no idea," she said, truthfully. "But I'm starving. Let's go to breakfast."

The four of them walked out of the room, Sophie chewing on her bottom lip the whole time. What had gotten into Emma? And why would she need to talk to Madame? Worse, why hadn't she told Sophie about it?

The girls reached the second floor and walked down the hallway's long, bloodred, velvety carpet, which made the space imposing at any time of day. The candle-shaped electric lights on the walls didn't help—all they did was throw weird shadows all around. Sophie got a chill passing through.

As they reached the top of the huge staircase that led down to the lobby and dining room, Sophie stopped.

"I'm going to go see if Emma's all right."

Ophelia shrugged and Kayley nodded. Madeleine put her hand on Sophie's shoulder. "I hope she is."

Sophie squeezed Madeleine's hand, suddenly even more worried about Emma. It wasn't like her sister to go running off. Something had to be really wrong.

She walked back down the hall, toward Emma's room near the staircase. As she prepared to turn the handle on Emma's door, something made her change her mind. She thought she felt a breeze from the staircase up to the third floor, and without thinking, she headed up the stairs.

Past the ballet studio, Sophie heard murmuring coming from one of the classrooms. The studio was dark now, and as Sophie passed it, she could still hear the ghosts of pointe shoes banging on the floor. The murmurs got louder: two separate voices, a boy and a girl. Sophie walked toward the noise.

As she got closer, she heard sobbing. And between the sobs, she heard her name. The words starting taking shape, and then she heard it.

Emma's voice.

"But I still don't know what to do about Sophie. What should I tell her?"

Sophie tiptoed closer to the classroom doorway.

And the worst thing she could imagine happened. She heard Trey's voice. "Tell her we're dating. She's your sister. She'll have to understand."

Emma's voice turned to sobs again. "That's just it. I'm her sister. How could I do this to her?"

Sophie's face grew hot, and she turned the corner to see Emma in Trey's arms. He was stroking her hair. Sophie's eyes blurred with tears as Trey and Emma jumped.

Emma backed away. "Sophie . . . ," she said.

Sophie burst into tears. "You asked a good question, Emma," she said. "How could you do this to me?"

She ran as fast as she could toward her room.

Chapter 2

Rounding the stairs, cheeks burning, eyes blinded by tears, Sophie barreled into someone. They both fell on their butts, and Sophie's head narrowly missed the last stair of the staircase. She wiped her eyes to get a better look at whom she knocked over, trying to catch her breath at the same time.

The girl, maybe fourteen or fifteen, had long red hair and pale, pale skin with gigantic blue eyes. She was faint and tiny. She wore a blouse buttoned all the way up to her chin.

Sophie had seen her before. This girl was a pretty good dancer, if Sophie remembered right. Sophie could also remember classes where the girl would sit in the back of the room not talking to anyone. And here she had just mowed the girl down like she was nothing. For a minute, Sophie was jarred out of her own misery.

"Are you OK?" she asked, getting up and rubbing her behind. Her tailbone hurt, and she imagined the girl in front of her hurt twice as bad, since she was half as big.

The girl nodded and said in a small voice, "Yeah. Sorry. I heard voices."

Sophie remembered why she had been running. She sniffled and said, "Look, I'm sorry, but I have to go."

Sophie wiped at her eyes and started down the hall again, the bloodred carpet and shadows matching her mood perfectly.

"Sophie, wait."

Sophie turned and saw Emma coming down the stairs. Even from her viewpoint, she could see the telltale signs that Emma had been crying. How many times had they cried together? Emma's cheeks always got bright red, yet she somehow still managed to look pretty.

Behind Emma, at the top of the stairs, half in and half out of the shadows, stood Trey. Sophie's body felt like it was on fire, and not in a good way. She was ashamed that Trey knew she liked him. Ashamed that he didn't like her back. And ashamed that she couldn't control her emotions enough to keep it all inside.

She never could keep things back.

She put her finger out at Emma. "You stay away from me!"

Sophie could hear soft chatter coming from the end of the upstairs hallway. She flipped around and moved toward the voices, hoping to reach her room before the whole ballet company came up from the dining hall. The last thing she needed was for everyone to see her crying.

She walked faster down the hall and heard Emma cry out, "Sophie. Stop. Let's just talk for a minute."

A sound came from her throat, something she didn't even recognize. It was half disbelieving girl and half wounded animal. The tears started to come in earnest again.

All her life it had been Emma and Sophie. She had always protected her sister, always made sure Emma wouldn't get hurt. She'd push Emma when she needed it and stand in front of her if someone came after her. She was Emma's twin sister, and she'd do anything for her. She'd die for her.

But evidently, Emma didn't feel the same way. Emma couldn't care less about her. She had known about Trey and had listened to Sophie go on like an idiot. She had seen the hearts Sophie doodled, seen Sophie add Trey's last name to her first.

Now, Sophie just felt like a fool. Emma and Trey probably laughed about her behind her back.

As she gained momentum down the hall, Sophie's sadness turned to anger. How could she? After everything they'd been through, everything Sophie had done for her?

Emma called out again, more urgently, "Sophie! Can you please just stop?"

Sophie spotted her room. Just four more doors to go. She sped up.

As she reached her doorknob, a hand grabbed her arm. She spun around and faced Emma.

"Sophie, I'm so sorry. You don't understand. Please let me explain."

"Oh, I think everything is pretty clear." Sophie's voice was shaky. She swallowed her anger.

"I didn't mean to hurt you, Sophie," Emma said. "This just . . . happened."

Sophie watched people gather at the top of the stairs, just out from dinner. But she could only see them through a red haze. Fury shot through her like a shooting star. All she could think of was how best to hurt Emma.

Like Emma had hurt her.

"I bet this just *happened*," Sophie shouted. "I bet you didn't have *anything* to do with it, did you? Because you don't do *anything*, Emma, right? You never take risks, you never speak up . . . I've had to do everything for you! And this is how you decide to finally quit being a doormat, huh? Well, it worked. You've walked right over me."

Sophie put her key in the lock and turned. Emma, face streaked with tears, grabbed her arm again.

"Sophie," she sobbed.

Sophie jerked her arm away and opened her door. "You just wait, Emma. You'll get what you deserve. Until then, don't talk to me."

She knew she was being harsh, and she didn't care. She wondered briefly about how many people had just seen her outburst, but the thought left her mind almost as fast as it came.

She turned around and slammed the door. Right in her sister's face.

Chapter 3

The next morning, Sophie did not go to ballet class. The thought of facing her sister, facing Trey, facing anyone who saw her go ballistic yesterday was just too much to bear. Instead, she lay in bed in her frolicking-kitten pajamas and stared out her window.

The day was gray and cloudy, just like Sophie's mood. The snow outside made everything look blank and lonely.

Just like Sophie.

She already missed her sister. Ordinarily, who would be the first person to console Sophie after something like this? Emma. Emma might not have been very brave or very confrontational, but Emma made things all right. She just always made you feel better. A tear slipped down Sophie's cheek. She was sad about Trey but much, much sadder about losing her twin. She felt like a part of her soul had been torn away.

She heard a knock at the door and jumped. It was already eight thirty—she'd been rolling around in bed for two hours, all through ballet class. She considered ignoring the knock but thought for a second that it might be Madame Puant, and Sophie didn't want to deal with Madame's wrath. She stood up and caught a glimpse of herself in the mirror. Her dark hair was disheveled and sticking up everywhere, her brown eyes swollen. She wouldn't be winning any beauty contests today. But she couldn't have cared any less.

Sophie opened the door and breathed a sigh of relief, although she felt disappointed at the same time. It wasn't Madame Puant, thank goodness. But it also wasn't Emma. Sure, Sophie didn't want to talk to her sister, but she still wanted her to beg for forgiveness. Instead, Madeleine, Ophelia, and Kayley stood in the doorway.

Madeleine held out a wrapped croissant and a yogurt. "Since you missed breakfast, we thought we'd bring it to you."

Sophie almost cried. Madeleine reminded her most of Emma—they were both unfailingly kind.

Ophelia pushed past her, and Kayley sauntered in too, loudly chewing gum. Sophie took the croissant and yogurt from Madeleine and smiled at her. Madeleine's smile back was warm and full of empathy. Sophie closed her door.

Kayley had plopped herself on the dressing table chair and sat playing with Sophie's hairbrushes and various containers of hair goop. Sophie swooped past her and smacked her hand. Kayley grinned, putting her hands up in an "I surrender" pose. Ophelia sat on the edge of the bed, legs crossed.

"So, freak out much?" Ophelia said, examining a fingernail.

Sophie knew that this was Ophelia's way of asking if she was OK. Ophelia wasn't good with emotions. Neither was Kayley, but that was mostly because she was lazy, not because they made her uncomfortable.

Madeleine jumped in. "Class wasn't the same without you."

Without warning, tears began leaking from Sophie's eyes. She wiped them away and grabbed a Kleenex sitting on the dressing table. She blew her nose as Kayley awkwardly patted her thigh. Madeleine came over and wrapped her in a hug. Sophie cried for another good five minutes.

Once Sophie was cried out, Ophelia said, "Class is in twenty minutes. Do you want to tell us what's going on? Emma was in ballet practice, but she was even less talkative than normal, if that's possible. She just stayed by herself in the corner. She probably only came to see if you were there. And she danced like crap."

Kayley threw a comb at Ophelia. "Well, she did!" Ophelia said.

Sophie sniffled. "It's nothing," she said, her voice congested-sounding and hoarse. "Just complete and utter twin betrayal, that's all."

She sat on the bed next to Ophelia. "Emma and Trey are going out," she said miserably.

When Sophie looked up, everyone was looking at her with confused expressions. She realized she had only told Emma about her crush. Because she had trusted Emma the most.

"Yeah, and?" Ophelia said. "So what?"

Kayley said, "Are you afraid the other half of your brain won't give you as much time now, Sophie?"

Madeleine threw Kayley a dirty look. Kayley chewed her gum and looked down at the floor.

"Well, yeah, that's part of it," Sophie said. "But it's way worse than that. I liked Trey, and Emma knew it. And she swooped in and took him!"

Kayley let out a low, long whistle. "Yeah, that's low."

Madeleine knelt down and grabbed Sophie's hand. "That undoubtedly sucks, Sophie. And she shouldn't have done that."

Sophie felt wary—Madeleine's tone of voice said she'd be adding something that Sophie probably wouldn't like.

Madeleine's brown-yellow eyes got big. "But, Sophie, isn't part of you a little happy for her? If your twin and best friend is happy? I know she's miserable without you."

Sophie flung her hand away from Madeleine. "Good!" she said and stood up. She was energized by the anger, and it felt good. Madeleine stood up too, to avoid being run over. She backed up against the wall, looking slightly alarmed at Sophie.

Sophie marched to the closet and grabbed some clothes for school. "She should feel miserable. She's been awful! I would never do something like this to her."

She started putting pants on, hastily, not caring what they looked like, as long as they weren't pajama bottoms. She stomped over to her dressing table and grabbed a ponytail holder, reaching around Kayley, who leaned back out of the way.

Wrapping her hair in a messy bun, Sophie

turned to face all of her friends. "I'll just say it. She is going to be sorry for this. I will never forgive her. She's dead to me."

Chapter 4

Sophie grabbed her books and marched out of the room into the always-dark hallway. Her anger started to sputter out. For the billionth time in two days, she felt tears in her eyes.

No way could she make it through an entire day of academic classes.

The academy was so small that everyone was with everyone else all day. She couldn't avoid Emma and Trey completely, but she could make a darn good effort.

She would have to go to afternoon ballet practice—Madame didn't look fondly on students who missed those classes unless they were deathly ill. Sophie was sure she was already in trouble for missing the morning practice.

She trudged to the nurse's station and walked in. Nurse John was there, tending to another student. She did a double take—it was the same girl that she had run into. Chloe something or other. Sophie hoped the girl wasn't seeing Nurse John because of their encounter earlier.

Sophie tried to catch Chloe-or-whatever's eye to mouth "sorry" again, but Nurse John blocked her view. Soon he'd be coming over to her. She'd have to rearrange her face to look sick. She looked down at the floor and held her stomach.

Before greeting Sophie, Nurse John asked, "Did you have breakfast?"

He was convinced all ballet dancers didn't eat enough. There were some, Sophie knew, that didn't. And Ophelia had almost killed herself through just that sort of habit. But most dancers Sophie knew ate like horses. They just had too much physical activity to do and couldn't survive without eating.

Sophie's stomach growled. She realized she hadn't touched the croissant or yogurt her friends had brought her. Nurse John heard the growl and pressed his mouth in a thin line. Sophie knew the speech was coming—his standard "ballet dancers have to eat" speech—but she was too excited about the upcoming breakfast to groan. Even though she was depressed about Emma and Trey, a plateful of eggs and hash browns and toast sounded just about right. Nurse John was all about the protein/starch/carb combo. He turned his back, and Sophie sat down on one of the beds, feeling a little bit better emotionally and a lot hungrier too.

She glanced across the room and noticed the red-haired girl was gone. She shrugged to herself. She'd just have to tell the redhead that she was sorry the next time they had class.

While she waited for breakfast, Sophie started to feel bad about how angry she'd been with Emma. And about her morning outburst.

Madeleine had been right. There was one

tiny section of Sophie's heart that was happy for Emma. Because she knew, deep down, that Emma wouldn't have dated Trey unless there was some real feeling there. And that the whole thing was probably eating Emma up inside.

Which meant that Emma was torturing herself with horrible guilt when she should have been enjoying her first boyfriend.

Sophie sighed. Of course she would forgive Emma. She was her sister.

The smell of fantastic food wafted over to Sophie. Her stomach growled in response. Nurse John set down the food, and Sophie dug in, half enjoying every bite and half lost in thought.

She needed to do something special for Emma, something that said Sophie forgave her. Because she really did want Emma to enjoy having a boyfriend for the first time. And Trey had never once acted like he liked Sophie back— she had no hold on him.

Sophie decided that she would take the rest of the day before ballet class to let go of the idea of her dating Trey and to let her love for her sister take over. Her excitement for Emma's happiness could overpower the jealousy. Then, in ballet class, she'd go give Emma a gigantic hug. Everyone would see then that Sophie cared more about her sister than someone else. And maybe that would make Emma feel better.

A gigantic weight seemed to fall off Sophie's shoulders. It was a good plan. And without all that anger, Sophie felt light as a feather. She finished her breakfast happily and then waited out the rest of the day for ballet class.

***

Sophie had fallen asleep. And that was not a good thing.

She glanced at her clock: 3:27. Ballet class was in three minutes.

Bolting out of bed, Sophie threw on the first pair of pink tights she could find and found a stained leotard to put on. She wrinkled her nose. Well, she wouldn't be the best-smelling person there, but she could bet she wouldn't be the worst, either.

She hurriedly fixed her hair into a tighter

bun and then grabbed the bag with her ballet shoes and warm-up clothes.

The bad news was, she would be late to class. Madame considered anyone late who wasn't five minutes early.

The good news was, she would get a warm-up by sprinting up the stairs.

When Sophie arrived, all the students were already at barre doing warm-ups. She threw her bag in the corner and grabbed an open barre space. It wasn't one she normally used, but her place was taken. Sophie tried to look over the sea of ballet dancers to find Emma and Trey or even Madeleine, Ophelia, and Kayley, but she could only see the backs of their heads. She caught Madame giving her a dirty look, so she concentrated on warming up her muscles.

Plié, grand plié, relevé in first, relevé in second . . . The familiar exercises felt good. Sophie let her muscles relax into them. She forgot about Emma and Trey and her friends and just worked on perfecting her technique. After about twenty minutes, Madame had the students move the barres out of the room and gather for center work, then pas de deux practice.

As she came back in the room after putting a barre away, she ran into Emma. Sophie gave her a big smile, but Emma looked down at her sister's shoes.

"Emma—," she started.

"I don't want to talk to you!" Emma said, a tear spilling over her cheek.

"Emma, what's wrong?"

Emma swiped her cheek and shook her head.

"You know what's wrong!" she whispered urgently. Sophie watched as Emma's sadness turned to anger. "How could you?"

Sophie was completely taken aback. She knew she'd overreacted about Trey, but when all was said and done, she was still the injured party. Anger flared in Sophie, but she tamped it down and remembered that what she wanted most was for Emma to be happy.

She softened her eyes and put her hand on Emma's arm. "I'm sorry I yelled at you in front of everyone. I forgive you. I do."

She smiled at Emma and leaned in for a hug.

But Emma stepped back like Sophie's hand was a hot iron. "Well, I don't forgive you!" she hissed, a fire in her eyes that Sophie had never seen before.

"Excuse me?" Sophie said. It was one thing for Emma to be happy. It was another for Emma to not even feel bad about betraying her.

Emma slitted her eyes and walked away. Sophie stood there, baffled, until Emma stomped back toward her. Madeleine, Kayley, and Ophelia stepped behind Emma. Sophie could see that both Ophelia and Kayley had looks of disgust on their faces. Madeleine looked confused and a little sad.

Emma pointed her finger at Sophie. "I know what I did was wrong. But what you did was way worse!"

Meanwhile, Madame slammed her cane to the ground and said, "Divide in two groups, dancers."

Sophie shook her head. "What are you talking about? I said I was sorry for yelling at you!"

"Don't play dumb," Emma said. "You know

what you did. And all because a boy liked me and not you!"

Sophie's head snapped back like she had been slapped. Bewildered and hurting, she looked at the other girls. Kayley and Ophelia gave her dirty looks and turned their backs.

Madame Puant said, "OK, group one . . ." and listed off a sequence of dance moves Sophie scarcely heard.

Madeleine leaned in close to Sophie. "I am having a hard time believing what you did too. That doesn't seem like you. But you were so mad this morning . . . I just hope you can find it in your heart to come clean and make things right."

"Madeleine, for the sake of being thorough, what is it I did?"

Madame shouted, "Girls!" and she continued with her counting.

"It's one thing to say that someone's dead to you, Sophie," Madeline whispered. "But it's another thing to tell them you're going to kill them. And your own sister!"

She turned on a heel and walked away.

Sophie stood there, feeling like she was in the Twilight Zone. And wondering what in the hell everyone was talking about.

Chapter 5

Sophie chased after the retreating backs of Ophelia, Kayley, and Madeleine as they walked out of the studio. She had to get to the bottom of this "killing her own sister" business. Emma had disappeared completely.

"Hey, wait up!"

Poised at the top of the stairs, the three girls turned as if choreographed to give her a nasty look.

From the bottom of the staircase, Sophie

said, "You guys, I have no idea what you were talking about back in practice."

Ophelia crossed her arms and stuck out her hip. Sophie noticed that Ophelia's turnout was perfect even in that small, casual move.

"Seriously? You expect us to believe you?"

Madeleine and Kayley shared Ophelia's stare of disbelief. Even Madeleine wasn't tempered by any sort of empathy. She just looked sad and disappointed. Kayley blew a bubble and let it pop, loud.

Suddenly, Sophie was tired. All that crying, all that fighting, and now this. It had been a hard two days. Her sister was mad at her and dating her crush. And now even her best friends wouldn't talk to her. For something Sophie was pretty sure she hadn't done. Everything seemed to catch up with her at once.

Her shoulders slumped and she turned away. "I don't expect anything anymore. Whatever. Have a great dinner."

She walked down the hall to her room, slowly, feeling like the weight of the world was on her shoulders. She opened her door, and without even taking off her blue Uggs, she fell back flat on her bed. She felt like she could sleep for the next fifteen hours and be OK with that. But a knock came at her door. A timid knock, quiet and subdued.

She ignored it. She was too tired to talk to anybody. And anyway, it was probably a former friend who was going to tell her she was awful or a sister who was going to steal her crush and then inexplicably freak out on her.

Sophie heard a shushing sound as something slipped under the door onto her hardwood floor. Curious, she sat up and checked it out. A letter, plain and white. She got off her bed and picked it up, turning it over.

The envelope wasn't sealed, and she lifted out the paper inside with ease. Unfolding it, she saw, in magazine cutouts that looked like a vintage ransom note:

I BELIEVE YOU

She turned over the letter to see if there was more, but there was nothing. She opened the door and looked down both ways of the dark hallway.

Nobody.

Of course, with the thick carpet and a student body full of people who were light on their feet, the chances of catching someone sneaking down the hall were slim to none. In fact, during previous adventures, Sophie and her sister had counted on those odds. How many nights had they snuck to each other's room and had a slumber party?

Sophie sighed. Whatever this note meant, whatever person believed that she hadn't done whatever is it she was supposed to have done didn't matter to Sophie. What she wanted most desperately was her friends and her sister to believe her. She fell back in bed and crashed out.

***

Ballet class was brutal.

Not physically. Sophie welcomed the release of jumps and twirls and arabesques. Just brutal in every other way. Sophie wished desperately that she was back in bed and that this strange nightmare would end.

The minute she got into class, people started whispering. She had been late again—earning another dirty look from Madame—and had started her warm-ups like usual. But soon she noticed the stares, the hard looks from almost everyone in her vicinity. Even the boys were huddled around each other in one corner. At one horrible point, Sophie saw Trey look at her, say something to his group of friends, and then watched them laugh at her.

Her face burned. What was going on?

During rehearsal, she tried to get close to Madeleine, Kayley, Ophelia, and Emma, but they all seemed to be protected by an invisible fortress of mean.

The only soft looks came from the girl she'd run into the other day. The one she actually had caused harm to. When Sophie caught her eye across the room, the girl—Chloe, was it?—gave her a tentative smile. Sophie smiled back sadly. She now knew how lonely it must be for the girl. Except, Sophie would have loved to go unnoticed at the moment. The stares and whispers were going to kill her soon.

After class, Sophie meant to grab Emma or Madeleine or Ophelia or Kayley and make one of them tell her what was going on, but Madame Puant stopped her as she walked out.

"This is the second day in a row you were late. And you missed one practice entirely." Madame's eyes bored into hers. "One more lateness or missed practice and you're out of the next performance."

All Sophie could do was nod, because for the billionth time in two days, she was about to burst out crying.

She ran to her room and sobbed on her bed. Worst. Ballet. Practice. Ever.

Once again, a knock sounded at her door. Sophie bolted upright and wiped her eyes angrily. If the letter writer was in the hallway, maybe she'd finally get some answers.

She opened the door and almost fell back. It was Emma. In tears. For a wild moment, Sophie thought Emma might have come to make up, to give her a big hug, and to say they should start over.

Instead, she saw Madeleine, Kayley, and Ophelia come into view behind her sister.

"I'm not going to stop dating him, so you can stop with the threats already!" Emma said.

Sophie's jaw dropped. What in the world was Emma talking about?

From behind Emma, Madeleine said, "Sophie, this isn't like you. And none of us have wanted to do anything because we thought maybe you'd stop. But if this keeps up, we're going to have to tell Madame. And you *will* get kicked out."

Emma hung her head.

Sophie threw up her hands and said, "I. Don't. Know. What. You're. Talking. About. Can someone please tell me what I did?"

"You know what you did," Emma said. "You are the only one with the password to my computer and the only one I trusted enough to give a key to. And you were gone from class when the first note appeared on my laptop—which gave you all the time in the world to do it. 'Stay away from Trey/or you won't see another day.'"

Behind her, Kayley snorted. "Not even a great rhyme."

Emma continued, "But the one today..."
She stopped and sobbed. Madeleine put her hand
on her shoulder. "That one is just off the charts,
Sophie. How could you? I'm you're sister!"

Sophie tried to process all the information
coming at her. A tendril of worry was starting
to wind through her. Her sister was getting
threatening notes?

"What did the second note say?"

"You want a reminder of your handiwork?"
Emma said. "You want me to let you know I
really got the message? OK. Fine. You wrote,
'Keep hooking up with Trey/and you will die in
the next few days/I'm watching you.'"

"Seriously. That's terrible poetry," Kayley
said.

But Sophie barely heard her. Someone was
threatening her sister. Not just threatening her
sister but threatening her sister with death.

Before Sophie could say anything, Emma
said, "Stop threatening me or I will go to
Madame."

She let out a sob and walked away. Ophelia
and Kayley shot Sophie another nasty look.

Madeleine's eyes lingered on Sophie's face before she followed them.

Sophie didn't care at this point what anyone else thought of her. She didn't care that she'd been unfairly accused or that her friends weren't talking to her.

The most important thing, the thing that fired her up and made her blood run cold: someone was threatening her sister.

And she was going to put a stop to that.

Chapter 6

The tricky thing about following her sister, Sophie noticed, was that Emma spent a lot of time in public places.

Which was good if you were a sister being threatened but not good if you were a sister trying to do some discreet spying.

Despite the hard looks from everyone, Sophie was on a mission. She didn't miss any classes—easier to keep track of Emma that way.

Madeleine kept giving Sophie looks from

across the room—tentative, probing looks—and at one point, a very small smile. Sophie halfway returned it, but she was busy trying to suss out who could be threatening Emma.

During classes, she kept her eye out for anyone giving Emma dirty looks or anyone flirting with Trey. Every look, every sound, every movement captured her attention. She studied Emma. Her sister had big bags under her eyes, and her hair was stringy and dank. Clearly she hadn't been sleeping. And her already sharp cheekbones stuck out even farther.

Sophie was furious—someone was making Emma miserable. Sophie kept on high alert.

But by midday, she hadn't noticed anything different among the rest of the student body.

Except that everyone thought she was psycho.

Sophie racked her brain. Was there anyone at all who had a crush on Trey besides her? The problem with the 4–1 girl-guy ratio was that half a dozen girls probably held crushes. But no one gave herself away during any of the day's classes.

Before the second ballet practice, Sophie saw Emma break away from everyone else and go into an empty classroom. Sophie looked around to make sure no one was watching and then followed Emma quietly.

In the same classroom where Sophie had learned that Emma and Trey were dating, Emma and Trey met up once again. Sophie could hear them talking. She was about to turn around—Emma was safe with Trey, and although Sophie was pretty over the whole Trey thing, she still wasn't eager to listen to their love whispers—when she heard a loud crash of glass on the floor.

Emma squealed.

"What the hell?" Trey said.

Sophie peeked around the corner.

On the other end of the classroom, safely away from Trey and Emma, a glass beaker had shattered on the floor. Emma was crying again.

"I can't take this, Trey. Why do these weird things keep happening? And with the notes . . ."

Trey stroked Emma's hair. Even though Sophie had once hoped that she'd be in Emma's place, she was happy that Trey cared so much for her sister. Emma deserved someone who treated her well.

"I thought we knew that your sister was writing those notes, Em," Trey said.

Emma stepped back, chewing on her fingernail. Sophie knew that chew. Emma was conflicted.

"I don't know, Trey. The more I think about it, the more I don't think Sophie would do that. She may be mad at me, and she has a temper, but she would never hurt me. I think I just got caught up in the moment, thinking about who might've had access to my computer."

Trey moved closer. "It's a pretty weird coincidence that those notes happened when she was gone. And that she is the only one who has your password and your room key."

"Yeah, it all points to her. But, Trey, something deep down in my heart says there's something else going on. Sophie just wouldn't be that spiteful."

Trey took Emma into his arms and said, "Well, that's a beautiful heart you have, so I trust it too. Maybe you should talk to her?"

Emma sighed. "I should. But if she didn't leave those notes . . . Oh, Trey. I've been a terrible sister."

"Sisters forgive each other. Go talk to her and see what she has to say about the notes. And try to make up." Trey smoothed strands of hair behind Emma's ears. "I hate to see you so upset."

"I'm so nervous to talk to her. To even see her. If she did write those notes, it's horrible, but it's even worse in some ways if she didn't. I need to practice what I'll say in my room during dinner. Can we meet up here later, so I can run it by you? She's so important to me, Trey . . ."

Trey hugged her closer. "I'm always here for you. See you in a bit, OK?"

Emma nodded, and Sophie decided that this was a good time to move away. She walked back to her dorm room with a gigantic smile on her face.

Nothing else mattered: Emma knew. Emma knew in the deepest part of her soul—the part where she and Sophie were twin-connected—that Sophie wouldn't have made those threats.

Sophie vowed to keep watching Emma until Emma came to talk to her tonight.

For now, though, she'd let Trey take care of Emma. Maybe Sophie could let go just a little. Emma seemed able to figure things out for herself, and she had good people on her side. Trey seemed to like her a lot, maybe even love her. And with her jealousy gone, Sophie felt amazing about that.

***

Sophie endured dinner alone. She'd thought of going to talk to Emma but decided to give her some space like Emma had wanted.

As she ate, Sophie noticed Chloe—right?— at the next table, also by herself. She sat and picked at her food. If possible, the girl seemed paler and more pixielike than usual. Her eyes were huge and haunted. She caught Sophie's eye at one point and quickly looked down at her plate.

Now even Chloe was ignoring Sophie.

With a sigh, she decided to go up to Emma's room after all.

Sophie stood up so fast she made a scraping sound with her chair, earning looks from the whole dining room. She walked through the room and passed Madeleine, Kayley, and Ophelia. Madeleine made a motion to speak, but Sophie ignored her. Time to make things right with her sister.

A trickle of unease passed through Sophie. She had no idea why, but she felt like she needed to get to Emma right away.

She took the stairs two at a time and walked fast down the red carpeted hall. She saw Emma from far away. She was wearing her robe and flip-flops, carrying her shower caddy.

Sophie slowed down a little. Having glimpsed Emma, she felt better. No one else was around. Her sister was fine. Sophie walked a little ways closer to the shower room and laughed to herself. Was she going to watch Emma take a shower? She'd just wait to talk until Emma came back to her room. Her sister was safe.

Sophie turned around and ran smack into someone again. They both staggered back a little.

It was the tiny red-haired girl again. Was she everywhere?

The girl's freckles stood out in glaring contrast to her pale face. Terror was in her eyes.

"Are you all right?" Sophie said.

The girl shook her head and looked away. She seemed to be debating something. Finally, she turned to Sophie and said, "I think you should go check on Emma."

"Why?"

"Um," the girl said, "I think there might be an exposed wire or something in the bathroom? I don't know. Just a hunch."

With that, the girl turned and ran away down the hall.

Adrenaline shot through Sophie.

An exposed wire plus water equaled electrocution.

Electrocution equaled death.

Emma's death.

Sophie sprinted to the bathroom.

Emma had taken her robe off and was pushing the shower stall's curtain away with her foot.

"Wait!" Sophie yelled.

An alarmed, naked Emma turned her head as Sophie barreled toward her. But it was too late. In a half second, Emma would be stepping into possible death.

Sophie smacked into Emma right as her sister's foot was about to touch the stall floor. They slammed into the shower room wall, Emma's head smacking against the tile.

"Are you OK?" Sophie asked.

"Are you trying to kill me after all?" Emma shouted.

She scrambled up and put on her robe, glaring at Sophie.

Sophie looked into the shower stall. Sure enough, there was standing water on the floor. In the water sat an exposed wire from the wall.

Emma would have been electrocuted.

Sophie pointed to the wire and the standing water. "No, Emma. I'm trying to save your life."

Chapter 7

Emma's face went white.

"Wha? What in the world . . . ?" She sagged against the wall.

Sophie burst into tears. "If something had happened to you . . . ," she sobbed.

Emma took two steps toward Sophie and wrapped her in a big hug. She too began to cry.

"You saved my life. I'm so sorry for everything. I'm so, so sorry!"

Sophie hiccupped and said, "No, I'm sorry!

I should have never said those things to you."

"No, it was all my fault. I broke the code! I'll stop dating Trey. And then I—" She wailed and hugged onto Sophie tighter. "I can't believe I accused you of putting notes on my desktop!"

Sophie stepped back. "First, you better keep dating Trey. You guys look so happy together." Sophie wiped her eyes. "Besides, I'm *soooo* over him. He's yesterday's news."

Emma giggled and wiped her eyes too. Then she got serious. "I never want any guy to get between us. Or anything else."

Sophie nodded. "I missed you. So much. But this is how life happens. Other people are going to become bigger parts of our lives. And that's OK. Because we're sisters and we'll always have each other."

They both hugged each other tight again. Sophie started giggling once more. "We're drama queens, huh?"

A voice echoed through the bathroom: "I'll say you're drama queens."

Sophie heard the snap of gum and knew that Kayley had found them.

Kayley, Madeleine, and Ophelia stood at the shower room entrance, wiping away tears of their own.

The twins began to walk toward them.

"What the hell happened in here?" Ophelia said.

"Sophie just saved my life," Emma said grimly. "There's an exposed wire down there and a puddle of water."

Madeleine, Kayley, and Ophelia all gasped.

"Holy schmolies!" Madeleine said.

Kayley's eyes were huge. "Did you see it there or something, Sophie?"

Sophie remembered her hallway warning. "No, that little redheaded girl . . . Chloe—is that her name? She said there was an exposed wire. And I saw Emma go into the shower, so I sprinted to grab her."

"That fairy girl, the one who looks like she's twelve? Yeah, that's Chloe. So that girl saw the wire but didn't tell Emma?" Ophelia said.

Sophie shrugged. "I mean, maybe she was *going* to tell someone."

"Did she see Emma walk in?" Madeline asked.

Sophie shook her head. "I honestly don't know. She showed up out of nowhere. All I know is without that information, Emma would be dead."

The five of them shared a shudder. The shower room door opened, and one of their classmates started toward the shower stall by the far wall.

"Don't go in there!" Sophie shouted.

The girl looked at her quizzically and said, "Aren't you the one who threatened your own sister?"

"My sister would never do something like that," Emma said. "And I had better not hear you saying anything close to that again."

The girl retreated with her hands out. Sophie felt a warm glow of love spread through her.

Emma backed away and added, "Unless you have a death wish, I'd stay out of the shower for now."

Chapter 8

"One more time," said Madame Puant, her face a mask of confusion. She'd had the same expression for about forty-five minutes as the girls tried to relay their story to her. Madame had immediately dispatched Bert, the maintenance man, to check out the problem. Ten minutes later, he came back confirming the danger. The shower was now roped off, and an electrician had been called.

"I don't know how that wire got exposed,"

Bert kept saying. "It came through a crack in the grouting, but I don't know how a wire could just come out like that."

But the girls knew. Someone was trying to kill Emma. At a small ballet school, people had their favorite shower stalls and stuck to them religiously. That one was Emma's. Someone had arranged the wire there and had timed it just perfectly.

The thought made Sophie's blood boil.

"Madame," Sophie said, "Someone is trying to kill my sister."

Madame shook her head. "You have a fine imagination, Sophie, but who would want to kill Emma?"

Kayley sighed. "Whoever left the notes."

Madame said, "And the notes were left on your computer, yes?"

Emma nodded.

"Did you see the time stamp? Keep the documents?"

"No," Emma mumbled.

Madeleine, Ophelia, Kayley, and Sophie flipped their heads around to her.

"What?" Sophie said. "Why didn't you keep those notes?"

"Well, I thought they were from you, Sophie," Emma said. "And I wanted to think that, in the end, you'd never hurt me. I didn't want you to get in trouble. So I deleted them."

Sophie ran her hand through her hair and then said the words that had been bothering her for days. "How could you think I would write something like that?"

Emma's face got red. Madeleine rubbed Sophie's shoulder and spoke up. "I think we might have convinced her, Sophie, to be honest. In your room, you said Emma was dead to you. And then there were these notes that threatened death, and you were gone . . . and you *are* the only one who has Emma's key and her password. We're so, so sorry. You were just so angry . . ."

"Yeah, I guess I can see that," Sophie said.

"No, it's unforgiveable," Emma said. "Somewhere deep down, I knew you didn't. But I didn't listen to that voice."

Sophie smiled. "Water under the bridge."

"Ahem," Madame Puant said. "I hate to

interrupt this episode of *Sisters United*, but we aren't getting anywhere. I'm afraid that without any physical evidence, well . . . I have nothing to go on. A wire in a shower stall—a communal stall at that—does not a murder threat make. And without the notes . . . you girls understand my predicament."

She stood up, managing to look imposing even though she couldn't be more than five foot two. "That said, my students' safety is my number one concern. Emma, my inclination is to send you home."

"Madame, no, please. I'm not ready to go home yet!" Emma said.

Sophie knew that her sister was afraid of missing out on any upcoming performances. At the school, missing any time set you back months, sometimes years. Sophie also suspected that Emma didn't want to leave Trey.

Madame stared hard at Emma and sighed. "The last thing this school needs is another scandal. Even a hint of one could do damage. But I'm simply not sure the wire was prepared for you. This school is very old.

"You may stay for now, Emma. However, if you so much as stub your toe, I'm sending for your parents. I'll see that Bert makes his rounds more often and add more hall monitors. I'll also talk to all the teachers and see if we can't ferret out who the culprit is. Threats—however serious—are cause for expulsion. In the meantime, Emma, make sure you are with someone at all times. All times—that means even going to the bathroom. Sophie, you have permission to sleep in Emma's room until we get to the bottom of things."

Sophie saw a small smile pass over Madame's lips, as if Madame too was glad she and Emma had made up.

"Now, if that will be all, I have an academy to run and a shower to fix."

***

Halfway to Emma's room, Sophie stopped short. Kayley ran right into her. "Dude!" Kayley said as she climbed off Sophie's heel.

"Sorry," Sophie said absently. "I just remembered something important. Right after everyone got mad at me, someone pushed a note under my door."

"Was it a note threatening to kill you too?" Emma asked.

Sophie shook her head. "No. It just said, 'I believe you.' But it was cut out of magazines."

"Do you think that's the same person who left the notes for Emma?" Ophelia asked.

"Think about it, Ophelia. Everyone thought I'd planted those notes. Even Emma. Because it all fit. Almost too well, like someone was trying to frame me. So who would believe me, then? The person who actually *did* leave the notes for Emma."

Madeleine's face scrunched up. "But why would they bother with all that if they were busy framing you? I don't know, Sophie. That doesn't add up."

"It just seems right, though," Sophie said. "Maybe the person framing me . . . felt bad?"

Kayley said, "What kind of a person would go through the trouble of getting Emma's key, finding out her password, sending her notes at times when you didn't have an alibi . . . and then leave you a nice note saying 'sorry, dude'?"

"That is a lot of stuff going on," Emma said. "While we're at it, how did someone get into my room and onto my computer?"

"Well, let's find out," Ophelia replied.

They walked to Emma's room, and Ophelia put her hand out to keep everyone back. "Emma, you're sure you lock the door every day?"

Emma nodded.

Ophelia took a bobby pin out of her hair. "OK, then I'm going to try to pick the lock. I saw someone do this once on *True Crime*, so I YouTubed it to find out how. I've only had it work once . . ."

She put the bobby pin in the old, iron lock and twisted it around. Her tongue stuck out as she concentrated. Sophie doubted that Ophelia's measly bobby pin was any match for the iron lock.

But then she heard a click, and Ophelia's eyes widened. "I think I got it." She turned the handle and the door swung open.

"Holy crap," said Kayley. "Are you sure the other time this worked you didn't try it on Emma's door too?"

"Nope," Ophelia said happily. "This is gonna come in handy . . . ," she added under her breath.

"Oh great," Kayley said. "Now we have Ophelia the cat burglar. Time to change the locks."

Emma walked in the door, her face pale again. "So basically, anyone could have gotten in here."

"Well, any delinquent like Ophelia," Sophie said.

Ophelia shot her a dirty look, and Sophie grinned. It felt good to be a part of the group again.

Emma shook her head. "Well, that's freaky. I mean the delinquent part, not Ophelia." She went on: "But that still doesn't answer the question of who got into my computer. My password is pretty good."

"I don't think *EmmaheartsTrey* is a good password." Kayley looked for a laugh from everyone and flinched when she got to Sophie. "Sorry, Soph."

Sophie chuckled. "Seriously. I'm over all that."

"Well, what is your password, Emma? You'll need to change it again, probably, anyway."

"My password was capital *N*, lowercase *u-m-b-e*, capital *R*, underscore *674834125*, exclamation point, asterisk."

"Whoa," said Kayley. "Does that number mean anything to you?" Madeleine asked, daunted by the password.

"No, it doesn't mean anything. I've had this password since I came to the academy. Remember when that hacker got into some of the students' tuition accounts a couple years back? Well, no one got into mine. I'm super paranoid about that sort of thing."

Kayley picked up a jewelry box off the dresser. As she opened it up, a haunting melody played and a ballet dancer spun around. "So we're looking for a hacking genius lock-picking delinquent with murderous tendencies?"

"Who likes Trey," Emma added. "And who's been here more than once." She pointed to a letter on the hardwood floor they all seemed to have missed. It had gone halfway under the dresser.

Emma picked it up and unfolded it. In the same magazine letters that Sophie had received, someone had written,

STAY AWAY FROM TREY OR YOU'LL DIE

Chapter 9

Emma dropped the letter like it was burning at one end. Sophie picked it up and examined it. "Yep, exactly like the letter I got."

"No bad poetry this time?" Kayley said. "That's too bad."

Madeleine gave Emma a hug. "We *will* find out what's going on. I promise." She smoothed Emma's hair back until Sophie led her sister to a chair and had her sit down.

"I can't stay in this room tonight!" Emma said.

"Nope, you're staying with me," Sophie replied. "Do you want to text Trey and let him know what's going on?"

Emma looked miserable. "He already thinks this is somehow his fault. I don't want him to worry anymore or go do something stupid. You know how boys are."

"Boys," Kayley agreed.

Ophelia scanned the note on the bed, looking perplexed. "I wonder why the note *wasn't* in verse," she said.

"Jeez, Ophelia. I didn't know you liked bad poetry," Kayley said.

"No, seriously. Why did your stalker put the first two notes on your computer—a thing that is almost impossible to do—and this note is on a piece of paper? And without the bad poetry from earlier?" Ophelia sat up triumphantly. "Also, Sophie got a letter just like this new one. I don't think there is just one person making these threats. I think there's something else going on."

Emma said, "Oh great, I have *two* people after me? I mean, Trey is great, but come on!"

Ophelia shook her head. "No, I don't think it's two people. At least not living people. I think what we have here is a ghost."

Kayley thumped her head on the dressing table. "Not again," she moaned.

"No offense, Ophelia, but you *always* think it's a ghost," Sophie said.

Ophelia flipped her head to Sophie and said, "Well, no offense, Sophie, but the one time I didn't think there was a ghost, I almost died. I mean, let's just go through what's happened in the last year alone.

"First, a coven of crazy people try to 'break a curse' at the academy. And frankly, they weren't too far off the mark, because we all know this school has some weird stuff going on." The girls nodded, almost as one. "Then Kayley kicks up some curse because she steals some shoes."

Kayley ducked her head. "We don't need to ever mention that again, right?" she mumbled, fidgeting with a rubber band on the dressing table.

Ophelia ignored her. "And I fell in love with a ghost who was trying to kill me. So, excuse me if I am a little prone to think of every possibility."

No one could argue with any of what she had said.

Finally, Emma spoke up. "But why do you think *this* is a ghost too?"

"Think about it. Anybody could have written those notes. But no one could have cracked that password. And on top of that, what student would have known how to mess with the school's wiring? Even Bert was totally confused by that. So this looks like the work of a ghost and someone living."

Everyone was quiet for a moment.

Worry tickled the back of Sophie's brain. "Well, what do we do then?" she asked.

Ophelia stood up. "What else can we do? We go to the library. We find out what's haunting Dario Quincy Academy."

Kayley reluctantly followed her. "I think it would be easier to find out what's *not* haunting Dario. Here we go again."

Sophie knew exactly how she felt.

Chapter 10

"Shhhh!" Ophelia said for the fifteenth time.

The girls crammed up against one another, one after another, by the library door at the end of the third-floor hallway. Sophie could hardly tell where her body parts ended and someone else's began.

They stuck together because at nighttime, Dario Quincy Academy was no pleasure cruise.

At midnight, when they were sure Bert was finished with his third-floor maintenance tasks, the girls had met at the library entrance and stopped just inside the door.

Kayley said, again, "I just want to put it out there, one more time, that *I hate the library!*" She had had an unfortunate run-in with an evil book earlier in the school year.

"Yeah, yeah," Ophelia said. "I think the coast is clear. Kayley, where did you say that back room was?"

Kayley groaned. "You guys, I cannot express enough what a bad idea this is."

"This is different, Kayley," Madeline said. "We're with you now. We'll look after each other."

But one glance at Kayley's face and Sophie knew she wasn't convinced. Kayley set her mouth in a grim line and raised her finger to a dark area behind the main stacks. "This way."

Sophie felt a shudder go through Emma, who was pressed tightly at her shoulder. Sophie squeezed her sister's hand.

The five girls crept as quietly as they could across the dark tile floor, each of them waving her flashlight beams up ahead. The area Kayley had pointed to looked like the mouth of a giant monster. Sophie understood why Kayley didn't want to go back there.

Once they were closer, Sophie could actually *feel* the place. The room felt heavy and oppressive, and she was convinced that something was going to jump out at her at any moment. A small light shone from a window high above, but all it did was shed light on the thickest bunch of cobwebs Sophie had ever seen. The musty smell was almost overpowering.

This time Emma squeezed her hand.

When Ophelia spoke, her voice was subdued. "OK, Kayley. Props to you. How did you ever come here by yourself at night?"

Kayley said, "I know, right?"

With the squaring of her shoulders, Ophelia said, "Onward troops. The sooner we find something, the sooner we can leave." She swung her light at the bookshelves, and the five of them walked into the back room.

"Everybody take a stack," Ophelia said.

Sophie gathered her courage. It was just a library. What harm could books cause?

She chose the second stack from the back. She said to Emma, "Search on the other side of my stacks so we can keep in contact."

The girls fell silent as they looked, which only made the library creepier. Skittering noises sounded here and there, and Sophie kept shining her flashlight at the floor, convinced she was going to see a rat. Or something worse.

Wind whistled through the high window above. It seemed to whirl and eddy around the stacks, bringing goose bumps to Sophie's arms. She heard creaks and groans, and at one time, she swore she could hear a sinister laugh. She heard Kayley gasp too and wondered if Kayley had heard the same thing.

"What is it we're looking for again?" whispered Emma.

"I don't know," Ophelia said. "A history of things that happened at Dario Quincy?"

A voice from nowhere and everywhere made Sophie drop her flashlight.

"Well. I'm not sure you want to know, girls."

***

Every one of the girls shrieked. They ran out of the stacks and toward the library exit so fast that legs tangled with legs, and all five of them landed in a pile on the floor.

A light flicked on. A lamp from a reading table not far away.

Geraldine, the librarian, stood in front of them, laughing hysterically.

Ophelia was the first to get up. She brushed herself off, glaring at Geraldine.

Geraldine held her stomach and put a hand up. "I'm so sorry, girls. That was better than a Three Stooges routine. Now why is it you girls are back here? And past curfew?"

Sophie's stomach dropped. Being caught sneaking around after lights-out could mean suspension or even expulsion. The girls always seemed to be in trouble with Madame. This would not be good.

Geraldine waved her hand. "Ah, hell. There are worse things than sneaking off to the library for some books in the middle of the night."

Sophie felt her shoulders climb down from her ears. Everyone around her began to relax too.

"Just curious, though, what are you doing here? What are you looking for in this godforsaken back room?" Geraldine squinted at Kayley. "You aren't looking for that one book you borrowed before . . . ?"

"Oh no. No, no, no, no, no, no," Kayley said.

Geraldine looked confused and shrugged. "Is there anything I can help with? I forgot my phone here today, so I came back to get it. But while I'm here, I can always do my job."

"We're looking for legends and stuff," Emma said. "About Dario Quincy."

Geraldine eyed Kayley. "Another school project?"

Kayley looked down at the ground and shook her head.

"This one is a little more . . . personal," Ophelia said. "We're just interested."

Geraldine exhaled and pulled out her desk chair. "'Just interested' in the middle of the night, huh? Well, I do know a ton about this building and its history. Why don't you tell me what you're looking for, and I can tell you what I know."

The girls looked at one another. Sophie wondered if they should tell Geraldine the rest.

Sophie made the decision for the others: "Well, we're looking for any legends of a ghost. A jealous ghost that is out to kill."

Chapter 11

Sophie expected Geraldine to laugh, but she didn't.

"Oh. You're talking about Millicent."

"Who is Millicent?" Ophelia said. "What happened?"

"Well," Geraldine began, sitting back in her chair, "Millicent was a dancer here in the 1920s. The story is, she fell in love with a boy at the same time as her best friend. Back then, remember, boys and girls didn't share this academy—it was strictly for girls. But the Monsieur who was running the place at the time would bring in male dancers for classes sometimes. And that's where Millicent fell in love."

Sophie could hardly believe it. Maybe Ophelia was right—it was a ghost.

"Let me guess," Kayley said. "She didn't die of natural causes?"

Geraldine chuckled. "Oh, no. No, no, no. This was one of the worst tragedies in the many years of the Dario Quincy Academy. Millicent was about to declare her love to the boy—I think his name was Thomas—so the story goes, when her best friend beat her to it. Her friend—I forget her name—kissed Thomas on the very night that Millicent was going to make her move.

"Now, keep in mind, Millicent was already a little nuts. Again, so the story goes. She was one of those artists who was maybe a bit over the top, needed emotion to fuel her work?"

Sophie nodded. She knew those dancers. In a small way, she might have been one of them.

Geraldine continued: "But when Millicent

found Thomas kissing what's-her-name, she lost it. They were on the third floor, I believe, in what is now the old science room. Back then, though, it was like a parlor room, a place where all the girls would hang out and chat. Millicent found a pair of scissors and stabbed what's-her-name. What *is* her name . . . ?"

Geraldine's thoughts overtook her, but Sophie had stopped paying attention. She was looking at Emma, who had gone completely white.

"Emily!" Geraldine exclaimed triumphantly. "Her name was Emily."

But the other girls had turned to stare at Emma too.

"Thanks, Geraldine. That's really helpful," Emma said, her voice shaking.

"Oh, dear. I hope I didn't scare you girls," Geraldine said, leaning forward. She looked around the room, concerned. "This place can get to you . . ."

Emma started to regain her color. "No, that was an interesting story. But I think it's about time we went to bed."

Geraldine winked. "OK. We'll keep this between us then, shall we? You won't be in trouble for being out past curfew, and I won't be in trouble for passing on creepy legends."

The girls agreed, and Emma began walking out, Sophie close behind. As Sophie prepared to ask what was going on, Emma shook her head. "In your room," she said. The girls snuck back down the stairs and into Sophie's room.

When Sophie closed the door behind them, Emma collapsed in the chair. She'd gone from shocked to grim.

"Well, it's Millicent all right," Emma said.

"What convinced you?" Ophelia asked.

"There are some things I haven't told you guys. Like, every time Trey and I are alone, something weird happens. Like, something breaks or noises seem to come from out of nowhere."

"That's horrible!" Madeline said. "How do we get rid of her?"

"There's more," Emma continued. "Trey and I always meet in the science room. You know, the room where Millicent went crazy?"

"More like *stabby*," Kayley said.

Ophelia's eyes started glittering. "Oh, yeah. It's Millicent, all right. And I know just what to do. We use a spirit board, and we make her back off."

Kayley said, "A spirit board? We don't want to ask her questions. We want her gone! What made you think of a spirit board, anyway? After everything you've been through with ghosts, I'd think the *last* thing you want to do is talk to one."

"A spirit board is the only thing we can do that will help. I did a lot of research after the whole . . . incident I had. I never wanted to feel that way again. And damned if I'd let one of my friends go through something like that. So I've been researching ghosts."

Sophie sat on the bed by her. She recognized that look in Ophelia's eyes. Ophelia was on a mission.

"Almost everything I've researched," Ophelia said, "says that ghosts stay on the earth to relive things over and over again. Their old lives get mixed up with the living, and they get confused. Maybe this Millicent thinks Trey is like Thomas. You know—two best friends fall for the same guy . . ."

Had she really brought forth a ghost? Sophie wondered. Just because she'd had a crush?

Ophelia went on: "I think we somehow need to let her know that this isn't Thomas. That this isn't the same thing she went through and that she's not living it through you guys now."

She looked at Sophie. "We're all going to be involved, but you might have to be the one who asks her to stop. I don't know for sure, but I think this Millicent is living out what happened in her life through you and Emma—which makes you, her, and Emma, Emily. If sites I've been reading are right, we need to talk to her stat. Before this gets any worse.

"This isn't some girl who was sad," Ophelia continued. "This is a girl who committed murder. She could be really dangerous."

"I'll do whatever it takes," Sophie said. "No one is going to hurt Emma. No one."

Emma smiled through tears in her eyes. "And no one will hurt Sophie."

"Yeah, yeah," Kayley said, "this is all well and good, but where are we going to get a spirit board?"

Ophelia smiled slowly. "I thought you'd never ask. I haven't just been researching ghosts. I've been stocking up on ghosty supplies." She stood up. "Girls, come to my room and check out my new spirit board."

Chapter 12

"It has to be the third-floor science room?" Emma asked again. "This is where it happened. It's so . . . creepy."

Ophelia rolled her eyes. "Exactly. That's why we have to call her from here."

Emma shivered. "OK, I guess."

Sophie cleared her throat. "And, well, this is where I first saw you and Trey . . . It's like Ophelia said: she thinks all our high emotions agitated Millicent's spirit. This room is a double whammy. She killed someone in here, here own life ended here, and then we come along, years and years later and go all . . . dramatic . . . Well, I guess we sparked something."

Emma said quietly, "Yeah, I know. We talked about it. It's just, this is like our own private horror movie. Why can't you ever just ask a ghost to stop being mean from the comfort of your own bed?"

Sophie started to giggle, and the rest of the girls did too. Laughing felt good. Sophie felt some of the tension leave her body.

The five of them approached a table in the center of the room, placing the spirit board in the middle of the table. Just as Ophelia had coached them, each girl placed her fingers on the planchette. Sophie couldn't tell whose hands were shaking the most.

Huge windows lined the far wall, and the trees cast long shadows into the classroom. The full moon didn't help—the light just seemed to twist things around, rather than illuminating anything.

Ophelia lit a candle, and the girls' faces

brightened in the warm yellow glow.

"Great. A candle. In a science room. This'll end well," Kayley murmured.

"Shush," said Ophelia. "I'm pretty sure the gas in this room's pipes hasn't worked in years." She rubbed her nose and looked a little uneasy. "I think."

Kayley groaned.

Ophelia flexed her fingers, hoping all the time she'd spent researching would pay off. "OK, what we need is for you, Sophie, to try to get Millicent to come out. But first, we all need to concentrate and be willing to let a spirit come into our presence. When you feel the time is right, Sophie, you start talking. Emma, you stay between people at all times, yes?"

Everyone nodded her head, and Sophie felt her stomach twist with unease. She wasn't fond of the idea of talking to a ghost, but if it would save her sister . . .

The five girls lapsed into a thick, restless silence. And then, Sophie started to feel something.

At first, she thought she must just be getting

sleepy because of the candlelight and the quiet. But she realized that she was incredibly cold and that her brain felt foggy. She didn't know how, but she understood that Millicent was there.

"Millicent?"

The planchette started to tremble. All the girls looked at one another. Emma's eyes had gotten as big as saucers.

The planchette moved slowly and landed on the *YES* space.

"Is anyone moving this?" Kayley hissed. "Don't lie!"

They shook their heads no, and even Ophelia looked scared. The planchette had moved on its own. Or had been moved by someone other than the girls.

Sophie swallowed. This was real.

She went on: "The person you loved—who was he?"

The planchette moved more quickly, spelling out *T-H-O-M-A-S*. There was no doubt in Sophie's mind now.

Sophie got up the nerve and asked, "Did you kill Emily?"

The planchette shot down to *YES*. All five girls gasped. The force of the movement was scary.

Ophelia whispered, "You're doing great. Now tell her that this isn't the same thing, and she can leave Emma alone."

Sophie nodded and swallowed again. When she spoke, there was a small break in her voice. "Millicent," she said, "I know how you feel. I really liked someone too."

The planchette moved a little bit away and then came back to the word *YES*.

Sophie continued: "I'm so sorry that happened to you. You must have been so hurt and betrayed."

The planchette circled around *YES* once again.

"I can understand that you'd think this is the same thing happening, but I want to tell you it's not. I am happy for Trey and Emma, and I want them to be happy. Emma is not the same person who betrayed you. I want you to leave Emma alone."

Sophie expected a big reaction, but nothing

happened. All five girls looked at one another. The planchette just felt like a dead, plastic object.

They stood for what seemed like hours, Sophie moving from foot to foot, trying to get feeling back in her legs. But still nothing happened.

"So, did we send her away?" Kayley asked.

Just then, the crash of a hundred glasses breaking sounded through the air. Everybody ducked as glass beakers fell from their shelves at the opposite end of the room.

Though the crashing only lasted for a few seconds, Sophie felt like it lasted for hours. When the last beaker shattered, everyone stood up.

"Is everybody OK?" Madeleine asked, her voice shaky.

Ophelia and Emma said yeah in unison. Sophie nodded too, afraid to speak.

Kayley, leaning on the table, said, "Well, I guess that answers that question. Millicent isn't going anywhere, huh?"

And just as Sophie was going to answer, she heard a groan from the other end of the classroom—a very live, very human groan. Right where the bottles had broken.

Chapter 13

All five girls ran to the end of the room, Madeleine in the lead. When they got to the other side of the desk, glass was strewn around everywhere.

Sophie looked in the corner by the door, and she saw a girl crouched there.

"Hey! What are you doing here? Come out, right now."

The girl whimpered but came out. Sophie could see that it was Chloe, the girl she had run into days ago.

Chloe, who always seemed to be around.

Chloe.

She was holding her hand, and Sophie could see blood dripping down her wrist, droplets hitting the floor.

And everything clicked into place.

"Hi, Chloe," she said calmly. "You're Millicent, aren't you?"

Without saying a word, Chloe started crying. Ophelia looked outraged. Madeleine stood back and covered her mouth. And Kayley said, "Wha . . ."

Emma just shook her head sadly. "Yes. This all makes sense now."

"Wait, she's a ghost from the 1920s?" Kayley asked.

Ophelia elbowed her. "No, you idiot. She's just been acting like one."

"We need to take you to the nurse," Madeleine said. Chloe spoke through tears, "Please, please, no, I'm fine. Please don't tell! I didn't mean to do anything!"

Ophelia stared hard at her. "Are you kidding

me? Not only did you threaten our friend, and you set up *an exposed wire to try to kill her!*"

Chloe's eyes were desperate. "Please, I didn't do anything with any wire! I swear! I just . . . I knew *she* had set it up. That's why I said something. I never wanted Emma to get hurt!"

Sophie grabbed Ophelia's arm. Chloe did look truly terrified, she thought.

"She's right," Sophie said. "She did warn me. I think we should take her to the nurse, but not tell Madame."

Ophelia looked at Sophie like she was crazy.

Emma chimed in: "Yes, I agree." She looked at Chloe kindly. "You're new here, aren't you?"

Chloe nodded her head.

"It's hard when you first start," Emma continued. "Let's just forget this ever happened and move on, OK?"

Chloe's face collapsed in relief. Sophie stepped up to the girl and stuck her finger in Chloe's chest. "If you *ever, ever, ever* try to hurt my sister again—or any of my friends for that matter—you'll be sorry. Got it?"

Chloe nodded, her eyes huge.

Sophie went on, the hard edge in her voice beginning to soften: "So how did you move the planchette? It really felt like there was a ghost at work. Did you use magnets or something?"

Chloe looked bewildered, but before she replied, Kayley butted in. "I'm glad we're all done with the threats and all, but we need to get out of here, before Bert or Madame comes in here."

Madeleine blew out the candle, and Ophelia grabbed the spirit board, both of their faces still white.

On the way out, Sophie grabbed Ophelia's arm.

"Thank you," Sophie said. She knew that it had probably been hard for Ophelia to admit she'd been researching ghosts. Ophelia's tendency was to pretend nothing bad ever happened to her, and the research was definitely a sign that Ophelia was still troubled by the brush with the supernatural she'd had earlier in the term.

Ophelia's big eyes reached Sophie's. She seemed as though she was about to say something when the girls heard murmurs of teachers' voices drifting in from the hall.

Kayley said, "Let's go!"

They only had seconds to get out of the room and to slip down the stairs without being seen. Emma and Sophie flanked Chloe, helping her hold her hand so it wouldn't bleed all over. Voices gasped at the bottle wreckage just as the girls hit the stairs.

When they got to the second floor, Sophie said, "Emma and I will take Chloe to the nurse's station."

Madeleine nodded, her face pale even after the dash downstairs.

"OK," Ophelia said, "but come back to my room right away when you're done. We have something to tell you."

Sophie nodded and she, Emma, and Chloe began their walk to the nurse's station, the blood from Chloe's hand disappearing into the carpet.

Chapter 14

Chloe's hand was stitched up, she was eating ice cream, and she still looked miserable. The girls had made up some story to Nurse John about Chloe falling and cutting her hand. He'd looked dubious, but he stitched her up anyway.

"Chloe, it's OK," Emma said. "Sometimes we do things that are a little crazy for love."

Sophie and Emma had figured it out. Chloe had a crush on Trey too. This was why she seemed to be everywhere Emma and Sophie were.

Sophie was determined to sort out the details.

She asked gently, "Chloe, did you plant the notes?"

Chloe hesitated mid-bite and then nodded, reluctantly. "Kind of. One of them was from me, for sure. The one where I said I believed you." Her eyes shifted around the nurse's station.

"*One of them* was from you? . . . You knocked off all those glass beakers, right?"

Chloe put her ice-cream spoon down and a tear fell down her cheek. She shook her head.

"It's OK, Chloe," Emma said. "You won't be in trouble. And we won't be mad."

Chloe swallowed and looked at them with hopeless eyes. "If I tell you the truth, you just won't believe me."

Sophie laughed. "We're pretty open-minded. Did you see that we were trying to do a séance?"

Chloe fidgeted with the blankets on the bed. "I don't remember doing any of those things. I just remember what happened after. Or I'd remember what I did later. Like, with the wire . . . I don't remember touching it. I just remember seeing it afterward. It felt like . . . well, it felt like I was . . . I felt possessed."

Sophie shuddered. Part of her didn't immediately believe Chloe. But another part of her, after everything she'd seen and felt at the academy, well . . .

Emma said, "That must have been scary."

"It was! I don't know what happened! I think it's this school." Chloe shivered. "There's something wrong with this place. After the wire incident, I called my parents. Tomorrow is my last day here. I never wanted to hurt anyone." She began sobbing again. "All I wanted to do was dance."

Sophie nodded. "Yeah, this school can get you down."

She still wasn't sure what to believe. The answer flitted around the back of her brain like a butterfly, unreachable. And then she remembered and sat up. She had to know: "Chloe, did you move the planchette? Actually, did you know we were going to do a séance at all?"

"I didn't know anything," Chloe said. "All

of a sudden I'm sitting in a pile of glass, and you guys are yelling at me." She scrunched up her face. "What's a blangette?"

Before Sophie could respond, Nurse John came over. "All right, girls. My patient needs to rest. Out!"

He pointed his finger to the door, and Emma turned to leave, always one to follow directions. Sophie took a final look at Chloe, who timidly ate more ice cream. Chloe looked at her with big, haunted eyes, then turned back to her cone.

Nurse John nudged Sophie to the door.

As Sophie and Emma walked down to Ophelia's room, Sophie said, "Huh."

"Yeah. Huh. Do you think that poor girl is telling the truth?" Emma asked. "I *know* something happened in that room. Something . . . strange."

Sophie shook her head. "With everything we've been through, with everything we know from this house, none of this is completely beyond belief, right?"

The twins reached Ophelia's door. Sophie

turned the knob, and they walked in to find Madeleine, Kayley, and Ophelia staring at an object on the bed.

The other girls moved aside when Sophie and Emma came in, not saying anything until Madeleine spoke.

"We have to tell you something. Something weird. When Ophelia and I grabbed the spirit board, we saw this."

Kayley opened the board. The word *DIE* was burned into it. Sophie gasped.

Ophelia said, "I don't think Chloe is entirely to blame for everything."

After catching her breath, Sophie said, "No. It's Millicent. Oh my god. Poor Chloe."

"Poor Chloe?" Kayley said. "How about poor Emma?"

Emma shook her head. "Yeah, this has sucked for me, for sure. But Chloe talked to us in the nurse's room. She wasn't working with a ghost, not consciously, or even doing things and trying to pretend that a ghost was doing them. Millicent *possessed* Chloe. She didn't even know what was happening."

Madeleine put her hands to her mouth. "That poor girl. That poor, poor girl . . . So the ghost can move things on her own? Or can she only move through Chloe? I don't get it."

"It seems like Chloe did most of the things that needed physical doing, like the notes and the exposed wire," Ophelia said. "But maybe Millicent was able to gather up enough energy to knock off the beakers." She pointed to the board. "And write that."

Sophie sat down hard on the bed. She could barely bring herself to say the words. "Emma, what if Millicent had succeeded?"

"So this whole love triangle thing—it wasn't Emma and Trey and Sophie," Kayley said. "It was Emma, Trey, and Chloe? Which means Millicent identified with Chloe and possessed her. Not you, Sophie."

"I feel so bad for her," Sophie said. "She came here to dance, and instead, she got taken over by a psycho ghost."

At least Chloe was leaving the school, Sophie thought, getting out of harm's way. Maybe Millicent would go back to where she came from now that the agitation and the heartbreak were over.

Ophelia sat up suddenly. "How do we know Chloe's not still possessed?"

Sophie thought for a second. "She's leaving the academy tomorrow. She seemed to be herself when we left her. With Chloe away from here, out of Millicent's reach . . ."

Just then, a knock sounded on the door. Ophelia opened it and the handsome visage of Nurse John appeared.

"Have any of you seen Chloe?" he said. "I looked up from my station, and she was gone."

The girls looked at one another.

"Ophelia. Please tell me your research included possessions," Sophie said.

The quiet in the room was louder than any glass beaker falling.

THE DARIO QUINCY ACADEMY OF DANCE

Ballet. Gossip. Evil Spirits.

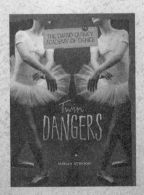

SEEK THE TRUTH
AND FIND THE CAUSE
WITH
THE PARANORMALISTS

THE HAUNTING OF
APARTMENT 101
MEGAN ATWOOD

THE TERROR OF
BLACK EAGLE TAVERN
MEGAN ATWOOD

THE MAYHEM ON
MOHAWK AVENUE
MEGAN ATWOOD

THE BRIDGE OF
DEATH
MEGAN ATWOOD

Check out NIGHT FALL
for the best in YA horror!

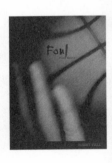

AFTER THE DUST SETTLED

The world is over.
Can you survive what's next?

About the Author

Megan Atwood is the author of more than fourteen books for children and young adults and is a college teacher who teaches all kinds of writing. She clearly has the best job in the world. She lives in Minneapolis, Minnesota, with two cats, a boy, and probably a couple of ghosts.